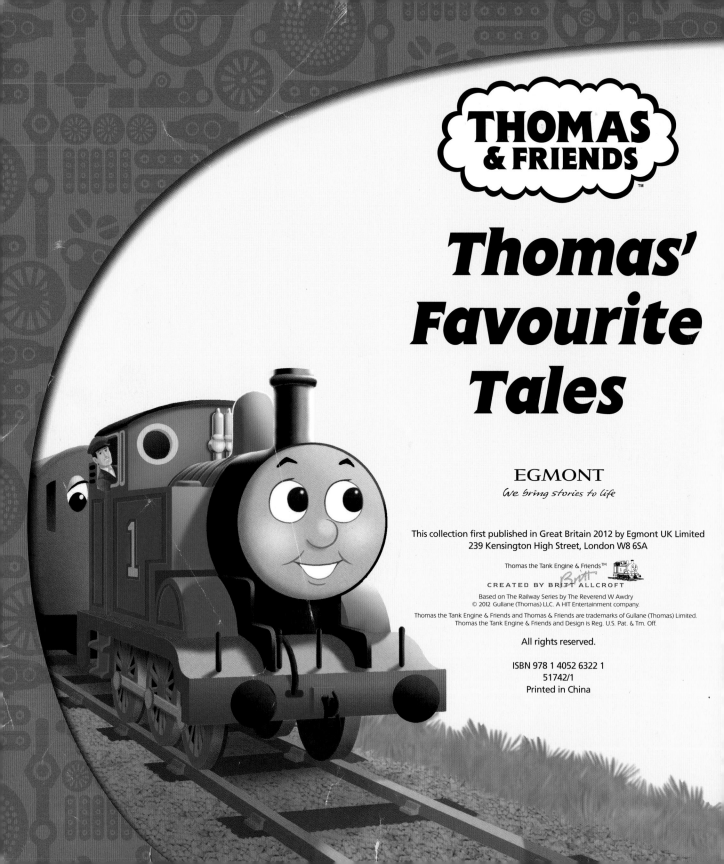

THOMAS & FRIENDS™

Thomas' Favourite Tales

EGMONT
We bring stories to life

This collection first published in Great Britain 2012 by Egmont UK Limited
239 Kensington High Street, London W8 6SA

Thomas the Tank Engine & Friends™

CREATED BY BRITT ALLCROFT

Based on The Railway Series by The Reverend W Awdry
© 2012 Gullane (Thomas) LLC. A HIT Entertainment company.

Thomas the Tank Engine & Friends and Thomas & Friends are trademarks of Gullane (Thomas) Limited.
Thomas the Tank Engine & Friends and Design is Reg. U.S. Pat. & Tm. Off.

ISBN 978 1 4052 6322 1
51742/1
Printed in China

Contents

Thomas

Thomas the Tank Engine had six small wheels, a short stumpy funnel, a short stumpy boiler and a short stumpy dome. He was a fussy little engine, always pulling coaches about.

He pulled them to the station ready for the big engines to take out on journeys; and when trains came in, he pulled the empty coaches away so that the big engines could have a rest.

But what Thomas really wanted was his very own branch line. That way he would be a Really Useful Engine.

Thomas was a cheeky little engine. He thought no engine worked as hard as he did, and he liked playing tricks on the others.

One day, Gordon had just returned from pulling the big Express. He was very tired, and had just gone to sleep when Thomas came up beside him.

"WAKE UP, LAZYBONES!"

whistled Thomas. "Do some hard work for a change!" And he ran off, laughing.

Gordon got a terrible shock. He decided he had to pay Thomas back.

The next morning, Thomas wouldn't wake up. His Driver and Fireman couldn't make him start. It was nearly time for Gordon's Express to leave. Gordon was waiting, but Thomas hadn't got his coaches ready.

At last, Thomas started. "Oh dear! Oh dear!" he yawned.

"Poop! Poop! Poop! Hurry up, you!" said Gordon, crossly.

"Peep! Peep! Peep! Hurry up yourself!" replied Thomas, cheekily.

Thomas usually pushed behind Gordon's train to help him start. But he was always uncoupled first, so that when the train was running nicely, Thomas could stop and go back.

That morning, Gordon saw the perfect chance to pay Thomas back for giving him a fright. He started so quickly that the Guards forgot to uncouple Thomas.

Gordon moved slowly out of the station, pulling the train and Thomas with him. Then he started to go faster and faster — much too fast for Thomas!

"**P**eep! Peep! Stop! Stop!"

whistled Thomas.

"Hurry, hurry, hurry, hurry!" laughed Gordon in front.

"You can't get away. You can't get away," giggled the coaches.

Poor Thomas was going faster than he had ever gone before. "I shall never be the same again," he thought, sadly. "My wheels will be quite worn out."

At last they stopped at a station. Thomas was uncoupled and given a long, long drink.

"Well, little Thomas," chuckled Gordon. "Now you know what hard work means, don't you?"

Poor Thomas was too breathless to answer.

The next day, Thomas was working in the Yard. On a siding by themselves were some strange-looking trucks.

"That's the breakdown train," said his Driver. "When there's an accident, the workmen use it to help clear and mend the line."

Just then, James came whistling through the Yard crying, "Help! Help!" His brake blocks were on fire and his trucks were pushing him faster and faster.

James disappeared into
the distance. Soon after,
a bell rang in the signal
box and a man came running.

"James is off the line! We need the breakdown
train – quickly!" he shouted.

Thomas was coupled onto the breakdown train,
and off he went as fast as he could.

"Bother those trucks and their tricks!" he said.
"I hope James isn't hurt."

They found James and the trucks at a bend in the line. James was in a field, with a cow staring at him.

The brake van and the last few trucks were still on the rails, but the front ones were piled in a heap behind James.

James' Driver and Fireman were checking to see if he was hurt. "Don't worry, James," his Driver said. "It wasn't your fault – it was those Troublesome Trucks."

Thomas pushed the breakdown train alongside James, then he pulled the trucks that were still on the line out of the way.

"Oh ... dear! Oh ... dear!" they groaned.

"Serves you right. Serves you right," puffed Thomas, crossly.

As soon as the other trucks were back on the line, Thomas pulled them away, too. He was hard at work all afternoon.

Using two cranes, the men put James carefully back on the rails. He tried to move, but he couldn't, so Thomas pulled him back to the shed.

The Fat Controller was waiting for them there.

"Well, Thomas," he said kindly, "I've heard all about it and I think you're a Really Useful Engine. I'm so pleased with you, that I'm going to give you your own branch line."

"Oh, thank you, Sir!" said Thomas, happily.

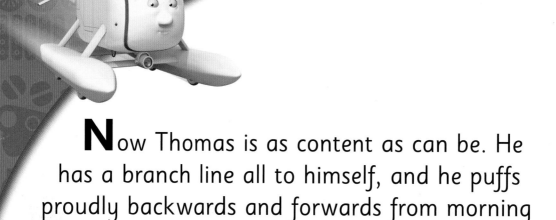

Now Thomas is as content as can be. He has a branch line all to himself, and he puffs proudly backwards and forwards from morning till night, with his coaches Annie and Clarabel.

Edward and Henry stop quite often at the junction to talk to him.

Gordon is always in a hurry and does not stop, but he never forgets to say, "Poop! Poop! Poop!" to Thomas; and Thomas always whistles, "Peep! Peep! Peep!" in return.

Edward

Edward was getting old. His parts were worn and the big engines called him 'Old Iron' because he clanked as he worked.

One day, he was taking some empty cattle trucks to the market. "Come on! Come on! Come on!" puffed Edward, as he clanked along the line.

"Oh! Oh! Oh!" screamed the rattling trucks.

Some cows were grazing in a field by the line. When Edward clattered past, the noise and smoke upset them. They twitched their tails and ran!

The cows charged across the field! They broke through the fence, and crashed into the last few trucks! A coupling rod broke and half the trucks were left behind!

Edward felt the trucks jerk suddenly. But he thought they were being naughty as usual.

"Those Troublesome Trucks!" he cried. "Why can't they come quietly?"

Edward had reached the next station before he realised what had happened.

News of the accident quickly reached the other engines.

"Silly Old Iron! Fancy allowing cows to break his train!" laughed Gordon. "They wouldn't dare do that to me. I'd show them!" he boasted. Edward pretended not to mind. But Toby was cross.

"Don't worry, Edward," he said. "Gordon's very mean to call you names. He doesn't know what he's talking about, cows can be very troublesome!"

This made Edward feel a little better.

A few days later, Gordon rushed through Edward's station.

"Mind the cows!" he laughed, as he roared along the line. But his Driver could see something on the bridge ahead.

"Slow down, Gordon!" he said, and shut off the steam.

"Pah!" said Gordon. "It's only a cow! Shoo!" he hissed, moving slowly on to the bridge. But the cow wouldn't 'shoo'. She had lost her calf, and felt lonely.

Gordon stopped. "Be off!" he hissed. But the cow kept walking towards him and mooed even louder! Gordon was scared and backed slowly away.

His Driver and Fireman tried to send the cow away. But she wouldn't move. The Guard told the Porter at the nearest station.

"That must be Bluebell," said the Porter. "Her calf is here. We'll bring it to her now."

"Moo!" bellowed Bluebell when she saw her calf. And she nuzzled her happily.

Gordon was very quiet on his way back to the station. He hoped no one had heard about Bluebell. But the story soon spread.

"Well, well, well!" chuckled Edward. "A big engine like you, afraid of a little cow!"

"I wasn't afraid," huffed Gordon. "I didn't want the poor thing to hurt herself by running into me."

"Yes, Gordon," said Edward, solemnly. But he knew the real reason why Gordon had stopped!

A few days later, Edward was late with the passengers for James' train.

"It's Old Iron again," grumbled James. "Edward always keeps us waiting."

Thomas and Percy were annoyed. "Old Iron!" they snorted. "Why, Edward could beat you in a race any day!"

"Really!" huffed James. "I should like to see him do it."

Edward heard James as he pulled into the station, but he just smiled.

Later that week, James' Driver felt unwell.
His Fireman was ringing for a relief Driver
when he heard the Signalman shout.

James was puffing away without a Driver!
His Fireman ran after him, but James was going
too fast! The Signalman had to halt the other trains
to make sure there wasn't an accident.

"Two boys were standing on James' footplate!"
explained the Signalman when James' Fireman
returned. "Edward is bringing the Inspector.
He needs a pole, and a coil of wire rope."

James' Fireman was waiting with the pole and rope when Edward arrived.

"Good man," said the Inspector. "Jump in."

"Don't worry, we'll catch him," puffed Edward.

By now, James was very frightened. He had realised that he didn't have a Driver.

"I can't stop," he wailed. "Help! Help!"

"We're coming," cried Edward. And he puffed with every ounce of steam he had, until he was level with James' buffer beam.

The Inspector carefully climbed out of Edward's cab and stood on his front. He had made a noose out of the rope and tied it to the end of the pole. He was trying to slip it over James' buffer! The engines swayed and lurched and the Inspector nearly fell, but he saved himself just in time!

At last, he did it. "Got him!" he shouted, and pulled the noose tight around James' buffer. Then he carefully climbed back into Edward's cab.

Edward's Driver braked gently, so he didn't snap the rope. And James' Fireman scrambled across and took control of James.

Edward and James puffed back side by side. "So 'Old Iron' caught you after all!" chuckled Edward.

"I'm sorry," whispered James. "Thank you for saving me. You were splendid."

When they reached the station, The Fat Controller was waiting. "That was a fine piece of work," he said. "I'm proud of you, Edward. You shall go to the Works, and have your worn parts mended."

"Oh! Thank you, Sir!" said Edward, happily. "It will be lovely not to clank any more."

James' Driver soon got better and went back to work. The naughty boys had got such a shock when James started moving that they decided to wait until they were much older before trying to drive a train again.

When Edward came home, he felt like a new engine! James and all the other engines gave him a tremendous welcome. Even Gordon let out a cheer! Edward was very happy that he would never be called 'Old Iron' again!

Henry

Henry was a big engine. Sometimes he could pull trains, but sometimes he felt too weak, and had to stay in the yard.

One morning, Henry was feeling very sorry for himself.

"I suffer dreadfully, and no one cares," he said.

"Rubbish, Henry," snorted James.
"You don't work hard enough!"

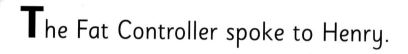

The Fat Controller spoke to Henry.

"You're too expensive, Henry," he said.
"You have had lots of new parts and a new
coat of paint, but they have done you no good.
If we can't make you better, we will have to get
another engine instead of you."

This made Henry, his Driver and his Fireman
very sad.

The Fat Controller was waiting when Henry came to the platform. He had taken off his hat and coat and put on overalls. He climbed onto Henry's footplate.

Henry managed to start, but his Fireman was not happy.

"Henry is a bad steamer," he told The Fat Controller. "I build up his fire, but it doesn't give enough heat."

Henry tried very hard to pull the train, but it was no good. He didn't have enough steam. He gradually came to a stop outside Edward's station.

"Oh dear," thought Henry. "Now I shall be sent away. Oh dear. Oh dear."

Henry went slowly into a siding, and Edward took charge of the train.

"**W**hat do you think
is wrong, Fireman?"
asked The Fat Controller.

"It's the coal, Sir," he answered. "It hasn't been
very good lately. The other engines can manage
because they have big fireboxes, but Henry's is
small and can't make enough heat. With Welsh
coal, he'd be a different engine."

"It's expensive," said The Fat Controller, "but
Henry must have a fair chance. I'll send James
to fetch some."

Henry's Driver and Fireman were very excited when the coal came.

"Now we'll show them, Henry, old fellow," they said.

They carefully oiled Henry's joints, and polished his brass until it shone like gold.

Henry felt very proud.

Then Henry's Fireman carefully made his fire. He put large lumps of coal like a wall around the outside of the fire. Then he covered the glowing middle part with smaller lumps.

"You're spoiling my fire," complained Henry.

"Wait and see," said the Fireman. "We'll have a roaring fire just when we need it."

The Fireman was right. When Henry reached the platform, the water was boiling nicely, and he had to let off steam. "Wheeesh!"

"How are you, Henry?" asked The Fat Controller.

"Peep! Peep! Peep!" whistled Henry. "I feel fine!"

"Do you have a good fire, Driver?" The Fat Controller asked.

"Never better, Sir, and plenty of steam," he replied.

Henry was impatient. He wanted to set off.

"No record breaking," warned The Fat Controller. "Don't push him too hard, Driver."

"Henry won't need pushing, Sir," the Driver replied. "I'll have to hold him back!"

Henry had a lovely day. He had never felt so well in his life. He wanted to go fast, but his Driver wouldn't let him.

"Steady, old fellow," he said. "There's plenty of time."

73

But still, Henry went quite fast, and they arrived at the station early.

Thomas puffed in.

"Where have you been, lazybones?" asked Henry.

But before Thomas could answer, Henry was off again. "I can't wait for slow tank engines like you," he said. "Goodbye!" And off he sped.

"Gosh!" said Thomas to Annie and Clarabel. "Have you ever seen anything like it?"

Annie and Clarabel agreed that they never had.

Henry was very happy. With his new Welsh coal, he could work as hard as the other engines.

Then one day, Henry had a crash and The Fat Controller sent him to be mended. Workmen gave Henry a brand new shape, and a bigger firebox, so he wouldn't need special coal any more.

Now Henry is so splendid and strong, he sometimes pulls the Express.

"Peep! Peep! Pippippeep!"
whistles Henry happily.

James

James was a new engine, with a shining coat of red paint. He had two small wheels in front and six driving wheels behind.

They were smaller than Gordon's, but bigger than Thomas'.

"You're a special 'mixed traffic' engine," The Fat Controller told James. "That means you can pull either coaches or trucks."

James felt very proud.

The Fat Controller told James that today he was to help Edward pull coaches.

"You need to be careful with coaches," said Edward. "They don't like getting bumped. If you bump them, they'll get cross."

But James was thinking about his shiny red coat and wasn't really listening.

James and Edward took the coaches to the platform. A group of boys came over to admire James.

"I really am a splendid engine," thought James, and he let out a great *wheeeeeesh* of steam.

Everyone jumped, and a shower of water fell on The Fat Controller, soaking his brand new top hat!

83

James thought he had better leave quickly before he got into trouble, so he pulled away from the platform.

"Slow down!" puffed Edward, who didn't like starting quickly.

"You're going too fast, you're going too fast," grumbled the coaches.

When James reached the next station, he shot past the platform. His Driver had to back up so the passengers could get off the train. "The Fat Controller won't be pleased when he hears about this," his Driver said.

James and Edward set off again, and started to climb a hill.

"It's ever so steep, it's ever so steep," puffed James.

At last they got to the top, and pulled into the next station. James was panting so much that he got hiccups and frightened an old lady, who dropped all her parcels.

"Oh, dear. The Fat Controller will be even crosser, now!" thought James.

87

The next morning, The Fat Controller spoke to James very sternly. "If you don't learn to behave better, I shall take away your red coat and paint you blue!" he warned. "Now run along and fetch your coaches."

James felt cross. "A splendid red engine like me shouldn't have to fetch his own coaches," he muttered.

"I'll show them how to pull coaches,"
he said to himself, and he set off at top speed.
The coaches groaned and protested as they
bumped along. But James wouldn't slow down.

At last, the coaches had had enough. "We're
going to stop, we're going to stop!" they cried,
and try as he might, James found himself
going slower and slower.

The Driver halted the train and got out.
"There's a leak in the pipe," he said. "You were
bumping the coaches hard enough to make
a leak in anything!"

The Guard made all the passengers get out of the train. "You sir, please give me your bootlace," he said to one of them.

"No, I shan't!" said the passenger.

"Well then, we shall just have to stop where we are," said the Guard.

So the man agreed to give his bootlace to the Guard. The Guard used the lace to tie a pad of newspapers round the hole to stop the leak.

Now James was able to pull the train again. But he knew he was going to be in real trouble with The Fat Controller this time.

When James got back, The Fat Controller was very angry with him indeed.

For the next few days, James was left alone in the shed in disgrace. He wasn't even allowed to push coaches and trucks in the Yard.

He felt really sad.

Then one morning, The Fat Controller came to see him. "I see you are sorry," he said to James. "So I'd like you to pull some trucks for me."

"Thank you, Sir!" said James, and he puffed happily away.

"Here are your trucks, James,"
said a little engine. "Have you got some
bootlaces ready?" And he chuffed off,
laughing rudely.

"Oh! Oh! Oh!" said the trucks as James
backed down on them. "We want a proper
engine, not a Red Monster."

James took no notice, but pulled the screeching
trucks out of the Yard.

James started to heave
the trucks up the hill,
puffing and panting.

But halfway up, the last ten trucks
broke away and rolled back down again. James'
Driver shut off steam "We'll have to go back and
get them," he said to James.

James backed carefully down the hill to collect
the trucks. Then with a **'peep peep'** he was
off again.

"I can do it, I can do it," he puffed, then ...
"I've done it, I've done it," he panted as he
climbed over the top.

When James got back to the station, The Fat Controller was very pleased with him. "You've made the most Troublesome Trucks on the line behave," he said. "After that, you deserve to keep your red coat!"

James was really happy. He knew he was going to enjoy working on The Fat Controller's Railway!

Emily

A new engine had arrived on the Island of Sodor. As Thomas puffed into Knapford Station, he saw a beautiful engine with shiny paintwork and gleaming brass fittings.

"Thomas, meet Emily," said The Fat Controller.

"Hello," the engines wheeshed to each other.

"Emily, go and collect the coaches so you can learn the passenger routes," said The Fat Controller.

"Yes, Sir," smiled Emily, and she steamed away.

The only coaches Emily could find were Annie and Clarabel. Her Driver hooked them up, and Emily puffed slowly and carefully along the track.

Annie and Clarabel grumbled all the way.

"There'll be trouble when Thomas finds out," whispered Clarabel.

But Emily couldn't understand why the coaches were so cross. She passed Edward and Percy, and whistled a friendly hello. But the engines just stared angrily at her.

Emily was pleased to see Thomas puffing down the line.

"Hello, Thomas!" she called, cheerfully.

But Thomas glared at Emily when he saw that she was pulling Annie and Clarabel.

"Those are my coaches!" he muttered, crossly.

Now Thomas was being rude, and Emily had no idea why. She chuffed away, feeling very sad.

Thomas was at Maithwaite Station when The Fat Controller arrived.

"I want you to go to the Docks to pick up some new coaches," he ordered.

"New coaches?" exclaimed Thomas. "But, Sir ..."

"Really Useful Engines don't argue!" boomed The Fat Controller.

Thomas was very unhappy. He thought the new coaches were for him, but he only wanted to pull Annie and Clarabel.

Later that day, Emily returned to the yard. Oliver was very surprised to see her pulling Annie and Clarabel.

"Those are Thomas' coaches!" he cried.

"No wonder he was cross," said Emily. "I will return them straightaway."

Meanwhile, Thomas was puffing angrily along the track with the new coaches.

"Don't want new coaches," he chuffed.

Emily was on her way back when a Signalman waved her down. Oliver hadn't cleared his box! Emily sped off to see what was wrong.

Oliver had broken down on the track crossing, and his Driver had gone for help.

Suddenly, Emily heard a whistle in the distance. Thomas was steaming along the track, straight towards Oliver. He would never be able to stop in time!

Emily quickly charged toward Oliver, and pushed him off the track, just before Thomas rocketed past!

Emily had saved Thomas and Oliver.
That evening, The Fat Controller had a
special surprise for her.

"Emily, you were a very brave engine!" he said.
"So, it gives me great pleasure to present you
with two brand new coaches!"

"Thank you, Sir!" replied Emily. "Thomas, I'm sorry
I took Annie and Clarabel."

"And I'm sorry I was so cross," said Thomas.

Emily was very happy. She had two beautiful
new coaches and a new friend.

Later that summer, The Fat Controller opened some new routes. Emily was given the Flour Mill Special.

"I have to do the Black Loch Run," huffed James.

"He's frightened of the Black Loch Monster," teased Thomas.

"Nonsense!" said James, and he puffed away.

"What's the Black Loch Monster?" asked Emily. "Nobody knows," said Thomas. "Black shapes move in the water, then disappear."

Emily was glad she didn't have to go to Black Loch.

The next morning, Emily collected the trucks from the flour mill. But they were being naughty.

Emily pulled as hard as she could, but the trucks made her go very slowly. Emily was late delivering the flour, so there was no fresh bread that day.

The Fat Controller was cross. "I didn't have any toast for breakfast. If you are late again, you will have to do the Black Loch Run instead of James!"

"I must get the flour to the bakery on time tomorrow!" puffed Emily.

119

But the next day, the trucks were being naughty again. They told Emily to leave before they were coupled properly, so half of them were left behind.

The Bakery Manager was very angry when Emily arrived with only half the flour. Emily raced back to the mill for the rest of the trucks. She was very cross and shunted them with all her strength. But the trucks had taken their brakes off!

They rolled backward and splashed into the duck pond! Emily was covered in a gluey, floury mess!

That evening, The Fat Controller came to see her. "Emily, you are going to take over the Black Loch Run!" he shouted.

"It might be nice," said Thomas, reassuringly.

But Emily wasn't so sure.

The next morning, she puffed sadly to the station. There were lots of excited children and holidaymakers waiting for her.

"I mustn't let them down," she thought. And soon Emily was steaming up hills and through valleys.

Finally, Emily reached the murky waters of Black Loch. Suddenly, she saw something move in the water. Her boiler quivered and her valves rattled! Then the water settled, and Emily saw what the monster really was.

"It's a family of seals!" she cried, delightedly.

That evening, Emily took Thomas to watch the seals. "Black Loch is a nice route after all," said Emily.

"Well, things aren't always what they seem!" said Thomas, cheerfully.

And both engines smiled.

Percy

Percy loved playing tricks on the other engines. But these tricks sometimes got him into trouble.

One morning he was being very cheeky indeed. **"Peep, peep! Hurry up!"** he whistled to Gordon. "Your Express train's ready."

Gordon thought he was late and came puffing out. But when he looked around there was only a train of dirty coal trucks!

"Ha, ha!" laughed Percy. But Gordon didn't think it was funny at all.

Next it was James' turn. Percy told James to stay in the shed because The Fat Controller was coming to see him.

James was a very proud engine, and thought that The Fat Controller must want him to pull a Special train. He stayed in the shed all day, and nothing his Driver could do would make him move.

The other engines were very annoyed. They had to do James' work as well as their own.

At last, The Fat Controller arrived. He was very cross with James. But he was even more angry with Percy when James explained what had happened.

When Percy arrived back at the Yard, The Fat Controller was waiting for him.

"You shouldn't waste time playing silly tricks, Percy!" shouted The Fat Controller. **"You should be a Useful Engine."**

Later that week, Thomas brought the Sunday School children to the beach. He asked Percy if he could take them home for him.

Percy thought that it sounded like very hard work. But he promised Thomas he would help.

The children had a lovely day. But by the afternoon, there were dark clouds overhead. Suddenly, there was thunder and lightning, and the rain came lashing down! The children hurried to the station.

Annie and Clarabel were waiting for them at the platform. The children scrambled into the warm carriages.

"Percy, take the children home quickly, please," ordered the Stationmaster.

The rain poured down on Percy's boiler. **"Ugh!"** he shivered. He thought about pretending that he had broken down, so another engine would have to go instead of him. But then he remembered his promise. He must make sure the children got home safely.

Percy set off, bravely. But his Driver was worried. The rain was very heavy now and the river was rising fast.

The rain was getting in Percy's eyes and he couldn't see where he was going.

Suddenly he found himself in deep water. **"Oooh, my wheels!"** shivered Percy. But he struggled on.

"Oooshsh!" he hissed. The rain was beginning to put his fire out!

Percy's Driver decided to stop the train in a cutting. The Guard went to find a telephone. He returned looking very worried.

"We couldn't go back if we wanted to," he said. "The bridge near the junction is down."

They would have to carry on to the next station. But Percy's fire had nearly gone out, and they needed more wood to keep it going.

"We'll have to pull up the floorboards and burn them!" said the Fireman.

Soon, they had plenty of wood. Percy's fire burned well and he felt warm and comfortable again.

Suddenly, there came a **"Buzz! Buzz! Buzz!"** Harold was flying overhead.

"Oh dear!" thought Percy, sadly. "Harold has come to laugh at me."

Bump! Something thudded on Percy's boiler. A parachute had landed on top of him! Harold hadn't come to laugh. He was dropping hot drinks for everyone!

Everyone had a hot cocoa and felt much better.

Percy had got some steam up now.

"Peep! Peep! Thank you, Harold!"
he whistled. "Come on, let's go!"

As Percy started to move, the water began to creep
up and up and up. It began to put his fire out again!

"Oooshsh!" shivered Percy.

Percy was losing steam, but he bravely carried on. "I promised Thomas," he panted. "I must keep my promise!"

The Fireman piled his fire high with wood.

"I must do it," Percy gasped. **"I must, I must, I must!"**

Percy made a last great effort, and cleared the flood!

"Three cheers for Percy!" called the Vicar, and the children cheered as loudly as they could!

Harold arrived with The Fat Controller.

"Harold told me you were splendid, Percy," said The Fat Controller. "He says he can beat you at some things, but not at being a submarine! I don't know what you've both been doing, but I do know that you're a Really Useful Engine."

"Oh, thank you, Sir!" whispered Percy, happily.

The news of Percy's adventure soon got back to the Station. Gordon and James heard all about how Percy had kept his promise and travelled through the terrible storm to bring the children home safely. They both thought he was very brave and forgave him for all his tricks.

Percy realised that, although playing tricks could be fun, it was much more important to be a Really Useful Engine!